# Comprehension

## Introductory Pupil Book

John Jackman

William Collins' dream of knowledge for all began with the publication of his first book in 1819. A self-educated mill worker, he not only enriched millions of lives, but also founded a flourishing publishing house. Today, staying true to this spirit, Collins books are packed with inspiration, innovation and practical expertise. They place you at the centre of a world of possibility and give you exactly what you need to explore it.

Collins. Freedom to teach.

Published by Collins
An imprint of HarperCollins*Publishers* Ltd.
1 London Bridge Street
London
SE1 9GF

**Browse the complete Collins catalogue at www.collinseducation.com**



Previously published as *Collins Primary Comprehension*, first published 1998; and *Collins Focus on Comprehension*, first published 2002.

10 9

ISBN: 978-0-00-741059-0



British Library Cataloguing in Publication Data
A Catalogue record for this publication is available from the British Library.

Cover template: Laing & Carroll
Cover illustration: Steve Evans
Series design: Neil Adams and Garry Lambert
Picture research: Gill Metcalfe
Illustrations: Maggie Brand, Rob Englebright, Bethan Matthews, Andrew Midgley, Lisa Smith, Shirley Chiang, Bridget Dowty, James Walmesley, Gwyneth Williamson

**Acknowledgements**
The author and publisher wish to thank the following for permission to use copyright material:
Walker Books Ltd for extracts from *Our Dog* by Helen Oxenbury, text copyright © 1984 Helen Oxenbury; and *Hiding* by Shirley Hughes, text © 1994 Shirley Hughes. Reproduced by permission of Walker Books Ltd, London SE11 5HJ; Gregory Evans and Egmont for an extract from *The Owl in the House* by Gregory Evans, copyright © 1997. Published by Egmont UK Ltd, London and used with permission; Egmont and Penguin Group (USA) Inc. for an extract from "The End/When I Was One" by A.A. Milne from *Now We Are Six*, Egmont Children's Books/Methuen Children's Books, text copyright © The Trustees of the Pooh Properties 1928. Published by Egmont UK Ltd, London and used with permission; Illustration copyright © The E.H. Shepard Trust and Egmont Books Ltd; and copyright © E.P. Dutton, renewed © 1955 by A.A. Milne. Used by permission of Dutton Children's Books, a division of Penguin Young Readers Group, a member of Penguin Group (USA) Inc., 345 Hudson Street, New York, NY 10014. All rights reserved.; David Higham Associates Limited and Emma Sweeney Agency, LLC for an extract from *Judy and the Martian* by Penelope Lively, Hodder Wayland, 1992, copyright © 1992 by Penelope Lively. Reprinted by permission of David Higham Associates Limited and Emma Sweeney Agency, LLC; David Higham Associates Limited for an extract from the poem 'Big Bulgy Fat Black Slugs' by Berlie Doherty in *Story Chest*, 1993, reproduced by permission of David Higham Associates Limited; Martin Skelton for an extract from *A Very Busy Day* by Martin Skelton and David Playfoot, copyright © Martin Skelton, reproduced with permission; and A P Watt Ltd for an extract from *Two Legs or Four?* by Dick King-Smith from *Animal Stories*, reproduced by permission of A P Watt Ltd on behalf of Fox Busters Ltd.

Every effort has been made to trace copyright holders and to obtain their permission for the use of copyright material. The author and publishers will gladly receive any information enabling them to rectify any error or omission in subsequent editions.

**Photographs**
p10, top: Busse Yankushev/Photolibrary; p10, bottom: DK Stock/David Deas/Getty Images; p21: Richard Orton/Photolibrary

Printed and bound by Printing Express Limited, Hong Kong.

# Contents


| Unit | | Page |
|---|---|---|
| 1 | Hiding | 4 |
| 2 | Our Dog | 6 |
| 3 | Owl in the House | 8 |
| 4 | Looking After Your Bike | 10 |
| 5 | When the Wind Blows | 12 |
| 6 | Gingerbread Man | 14 |
| 7 | Hippo and Monkey | 16 |
| 8 | When I Was One | 18 |
| 9 | Looking at a Dictionary | 20 |
| 10 | Judy and the Martian | 22 |
| 11 | The Three Billy Goats Gruff | 24 |
| 12 | Big Bulgy Fat Black Slugs | 26 |
| 13 | A Very Busy Day | 28 |
| Progress Unit | Two Legs or Four? | 30 |

# Unit 1 Hiding

Under a bush in the garden
is a very good place to hide.

So is a big umbrella,
or down at the end of a bed.

Sometimes Dad hides
behind a newspaper.
And Mum hides behind
a book on the sofa.

You can even hide under a hat.

Tortoises hide inside their shells
when they aren't feeling friendly,
and hamsters hide right at the
back of their cages when they
want to go to sleep.

When the baby hides his eyes
he thinks you can't see him.
But he's there all the time.

**Shirley Hughes**

## Do you remember?

**Copy these sentences.**
**Fill each gap.**

1. Where is the boy hiding?
   The boy is hiding under the ________.

2. Where is the girl hiding?
   The girl is hiding under the __________.
3. Which animals hide inside their shells?
   __________ hide inside their shells.
4. Who hides behind a newspaper?
   __________ hides behind a newspaper.

## More to think about

**Read these sentences about the story. Write 'true' or 'not true' for each one.**

1. Under a bush is a bad place to hide.
2. Dad is hiding behind his newspaper.
3. Mum is sitting on the floor.
4. Tortoises hide inside their shells.
5. The baby thinks you can't see him.

## Now try these

**Write a sentence to answer each question.**

1. Why do you think Dad hides behind his newspaper?
2. Why does the baby think you can't see him when he hides his eyes?
3. Where is your favourite hiding place?
4. What other creatures hide in shells?

# Unit 2 Our Dog

Our dog has to go for walks every day.
She stares at us until we take her.

One day she found a smelly pond
and jumped into it.
"Pooh! You smell disgusting!"
we told her.

Then she rolled in the mud.
"Pretend she's not ours," whispered Mum.
"We must get her home quickly and
give her a bath."

We made her wait outside the kitchen door.
Mum filled the bath.
"I'll put her in," Mum said.
"Now hold on tight! Don't let her jump out!"

**Helen Oxenbury**

## Do you remember?

| bath | mud | day | smelly |
|---|---|---|---|

**Copy these sentences.**
**Choose a word from the box to fill each gap.**

1. The dog has a walk every __________.
2. One day she jumped in a __________ pond.
3. She also rolled in the __________.
4. They took the dog home and gave her a __________.

## More to think about

**Read these sentences about the story. Write 'true' or 'not true' for each one.**

1. The dog has a walk once a week.
2. She barks when she wants a walk.
3. The dog likes smelly ponds.
4. Sometimes she gets herself muddy.
5. She has a bath in the kitchen.
6. The dog sits quietly in the bath.

## Now try these

1. Why do you think the dog would want to jump out of the bath?
2. Imagine you are the dog.
   Explain how you feel as you jump into the pond.
3. These instructions for bathing the dog are in the wrong order.
   Copy them in the right order.

**Dry her with a towel.**

**Rinse off all the soap.**

**Splash the water onto the dog's coat.**

**Fill the bath with warm water.**

**Lift the dog into the water.**

**Rub shampoo into her wet coat.**

Unit 3

# Owl in the House

Owl was out on his first ever hunting trip when a storm blew up.

A sudden gust of wind
made Owl lose
his balance and tumble
into the chimney.

Owl felt frightened, but
the house was warm and
calm after the stormy
night. He shook his sooty
feathers and flew off.

In the hall, Owl stood still
and spread his wings.
No wind ruffled his feathers.
There were no smells of trees
or grass, earth or rain.
So Owl knew the house was
locked up tight, like
a big sealed box.

**Gregory Evans**

## Do you remember?

**Copy these sentences.**
**Choose the correct word to fill each gap.**

1. A sudden gust of __________ made Owl lose his balance. (wind, rain)
2. He __________ into the chimney. (jumped, tumbled)
3. He felt __________. (warm, cold)
4. In the hall, Owl __________ his wings. (spread, cleaned)
5. The __________ was locked up tight. (cupboard, house)

## More to think about

**Read these sentences about the story.**
**Write 'true' or 'not true' for each one.**

1. Owl was quite young.
2. It was a stormy night.
3. Owl had been hunting many times before.
4. He flew into the house on purpose.
5. His feathers got covered in soot.
6. Owl was trapped in the house.

## Now try these

1. What do you think happened next? Write your own ending.
2. Pretend that you are trapped somewhere. Write some sentences about where you are and how you feel.

# Unit 4 Looking After Your Bike

A bike is a machine.
All machines need to be looked after carefully.

## Tips for looking after your bike

Clean and dry your bike
when it is wet or muddy.
This will stop it getting rusty.

Ask someone to help you
to check the brakes.
The brakes are very
important for your safety.

Be sure that there is enough air in the tyres.
When the tyres are soft or flat it is more difficult
to keep your balance.

Make sure the seat is at
the correct height for you.
You should be able to touch
the ground with both feet.
When you stop you don't
want to topple over!

Always wear your helmet
when you ride your bike.
If you fall off your head
must be protected.

Be proud of your bike, and
be proud of the way you ride it!

## Do you remember?

**Copy these sentences.**
**Fill each gap.**

1. If you don't keep your bike dry it will get __________.
2. Good brakes are important for your __________.
3. You might fall off if your tyres are __________.
4. You might topple over if you can't touch the __________.
5. You wear a helmet to protect your __________.

## More to think about

**Write a sentence to answer each question.**

1. Why do you need to keep your bike dry?
2. Why are brakes very important?
3. How can you tell if your seat is the correct height?
4. What might happen if your seat was too high?
5. What should you always wear when riding your bike?

## Now try these

1. Pretend it is your birthday. You have been given a new bike. Describe what it is like.
2. Make a list of the good things about having a bike.
3. Imagine you are about to go for a bike ride. Explain how you will get ready.

# Unit 5 When the Wind Blows

When the wind blows
Coats flap, scarves flutter.

When the wind blows
Branches groan, leaves mutter.

When the wind blows
Curtains swish, papers scatter.

When the wind blows
Gates creak, dustbins clatter.

When the wind blows
Doors slam, windows rattle.

When the wind blows
Inside is a haven
Outside is a battle.

**John Foster**

## Do you remember?

**Copy these sentences.**
**Choose a word from the box to fill each gap.**

| scatter | mutter | flutter | clatter |
|---|---|---|---|

1. When the wind blows scarves __________.
2. When the wind blows leaves __________.
3. When the wind blows papers __________.
4. When the wind blows dustbins __________.

## More to think about

1. Find a word from the poem that rhymes with each of these words.
   a) mutter
   b) scatter
   c) battle
2. The poet uses words that describe sounds.
   What makes these sounds in the poem? One has been done to help you.

| Sound | Describes |
| --- | --- |
| groan | branches |
| creak | |
| slam | |
| clatter | |
| rattle | |

## Now try these

1. What else happens on windy days? Make a list of your ideas.
2. What is your favourite weather? Say why you like it best.
3. Write three words to describe your favourite weather.

# Unit 6 Gingerbread Man

One day Gran made a gingerbread man for the children. As she opened her oven, up jumped the gingerbread man and off he ran.

"Stop, stop," called the cat.
"Let's have a chat."

"Oh no, not me.
No one's eating me
for tea," he shouted,
and on he ran.
On and on ran
the little man.

"Stop, stop," called
the bird. "Let's have
a word."

"Oh no, not me.
No one's eating me
for tea," he shouted,
and on he ran.
On and on ran
the little man.

But then the gingerbread man
came to a big, wide lake.

"I can help," said the old fox.
"I will carry you across the lake."
"Sit on my tail," said the old fox.
"Sit on my back," said the old fox.
"Sit on my nose," said the old fox.

**Traditional tale**

## Do you remember?

**Copy these sentences.**
**Choose the correct word to fill each gap.**

1. The gingerbread man jumped from the __________.
   (oven, cupboard)
2. First he ran past the __________. (cat, rat)
3. On he ran past the __________. (chicken, bird)
4. When he reached the __________ he stopped. (hill, lake)
5. A __________ said he would help. (fish, fox)

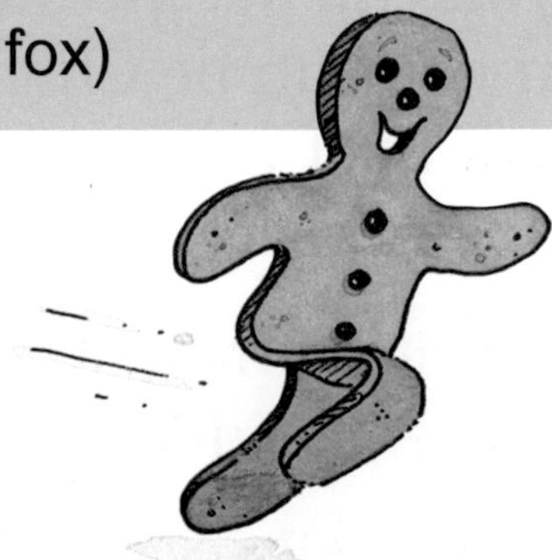

## More to think about

**Read these sentences about the story. Copy them in the right order. The first one has been done to help you.**

**The bird tried to stop him.**

**The gingerbread man ran past the cat.**

**He came to the lake.**

**The fox told the gingerbread man to sit on his nose.**

**The fox said he could help.**

1. The gingerbread man ran past the cat.

## Now try these

1. Pretend you are the gingerbread man. Write about how you feel when you come to the lake.
2. Why do you think the fox tells the gingerbread man to sit on its nose?
3. Write your own ending for the story. Try to make it a surprise.

Unit 7

# Hippo and Monkey

Hippo was the strongest of all the animals, so he said he should be Chief. The other animals didn't want Hippo as their Chief. He was too grumpy and moody.

"If I can get you out of the pool, then I should be Chief," said Monkey.

"If you can get me out of the pool, then you can be Chief," said Hippo, "But if I get you into the pool, you will be my servant – for ever!"

Off went Monkey to get a really strong rope. "Hold tight to the rope," said Monkey, "but don't pull until I shout."

Monkey ran into the trees with the other end of the rope. Monkey tied the rope to a big, strong tree trunk.
"Pull!" shouted Monkey. "Pull!"
"This will be easy," thought Hippo to himself.

All day and all night Hippo pulled, while Monkey sat and ate bananas, and snoozed!

Hippo was getting very tired and cross, very cross indeed.

Slowly he climbed out of the pool, to try to see Monkey.

Just as Hippo took his last foot out of the pool, Monkey ran out of the trees …

**Nigerian folk tale**

## Do you remember?

**Copy these sentences.**
**Choose the correct word to fill each gap.**

1. Monkey wanted to be __________. (chief, servant)
2. Hippo liked to sit in the __________ all day. (mud, pool)
3. Monkey tied the rope to a __________. (tree, log)
4. Hippo thought getting Monkey into the pool would be __________. (hard, easy)
5. Monkey played a __________ on Hippo. (trick, game)

## More to think about

**Sort the words in the box into two lists.**
**Two have been done to help you.**

**brown grey**
**huge fat clever**
**moody grumpy**
**small thin**

| Words that describe Monkey | Words that describe Hippo |
|---|---|
| brown | grey |

## Now try these

1. Why do you think the animals didn't want Hippo to be their Chief?
2. Imagine that Monkey is telling the other animals that he is Chief. What do you think they said? Write a conversation between Monkey and the other animals.

Unit 8

# When I Was One

When I was One,
I had just begun.
When I was Two,
I was nearly new.
When I was Three,
I was hardly me.
When I was Four,
I was not much more.
When I was Five,
I was just alive.
But now I am Six,
I'm as clever as clever.
So I think I'll be Six now
for ever and ever.

**A.A. Milne**

## Do you remember?

**Look at the picture. Copy these sentences.
Choose a word from the box to fill each gap.**

| presents | cat | cake | children |
|---|---|---|---|

1. There are six candles on the __________.
2. The __________ is under the table.
3. The boy hasn't opened his __________ yet.
4. Four __________ have come to his party.

## More to think about

1. Find a word in the poem to rhyme with these words. The first one has been done to help you.
   a) one … begun b) two … __________
   c) three … __________ d) four … __________
   e) five … __________
2. Write a different word of your own to rhyme with these words.
   a) one b) two c) three

## Now try these

1. Write a list of the five things you like best about birthdays.
2. How old would you like to be now? Explain your answer.

# Unit 9 Looking at a Dictionary

**ever** always, for all time

**every** all, one

**examination** 1) a test
2) a close look

**excellent** very, very good

**excuse** a reason for doing or not doing something

**expect** to think something will happen

**explode** to blow up

**eye** the part of the body you see with

**Ff**

**face** 1) the front part of the head
2) to look towards

**fact** something that is true

**factory** a building where things are made

**fail** 1) not to do something you try to do
2) to break down

**fair** 1) a show or market
2) blond or light in colour
3) just, honest

**fall** to drop down

## Do you remember?

**Look at the words in thick black print.**
**Write a sentence to answer each question.**

1. How many words begin with e?
2. How many words begin with f?
3. Which is the first word that begins with e?
4. What is the last word that begins with f?

## More to think about

1. Copy the lists of words and meanings.
   Draw lines to match them. One has been done to help you.

| Word | Meaning |
|---|---|
| examination | not to do something you try to do |
| excuse | the part of the body you see with |
| eye | something that is true |
| fact | a reason for doing or not doing something |
| fail | a test |

2. These words have been missed out of the dictionary entry.
   Which word would they come after?
   a) expert b) famous c) fade

## Now try these

1. Which words have two different meanings?
2. Choose a word that has two different meanings.
   Write two sentences using the word you chose, one for each of its different meanings.
3. Write a meaning for each of these words. Check your answers in a dictionary.
   a) acorn
   b) blow
   c) canal
   d) dislike
   e) enjoy
   f) free

# Unit 10 Judy and the Martian

It was the middle of the night when the rocket landed in the supermarket car park. The engine had failed. The hatch opened and the Martian peered out. A Martian, I should tell you, has webbed feet, green skin and eyes on the ends of horns like a snail. This one, who was three hundred and twenty-seven years old, wore a red jersey.

He said, "Bother!" He had only passed his driving test the week before and was already losing his way.

He was also an extremely nervous person, and felt the cold badly. He shivered. A car hooted and he scuttled behind a rubbish bin.

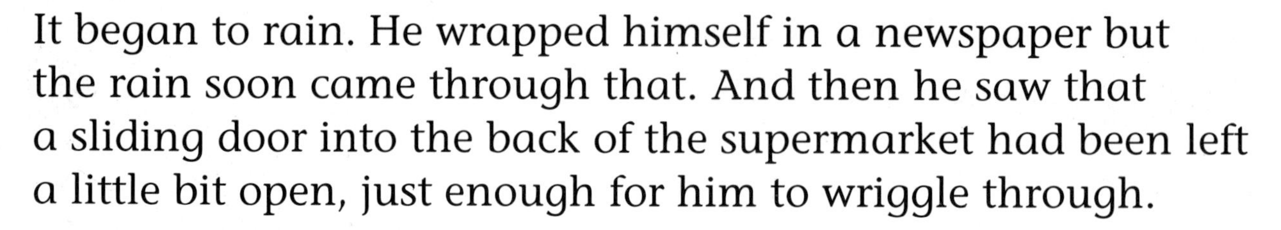

It began to rain. He wrapped himself in a newspaper but the rain soon came through that. And then he saw that a sliding door into the back of the supermarket had been left a little bit open, just enough for him to wriggle through.

**Penelope Lively**

## Do you remember?

**Copy these sentences.**
**Choose the correct ending to finish each sentence.**

1. The rocket landed __________. (in a car park, in a field, in a garden)
2. The Martian had __________. (red skin, blue skin, green skin)

3. He was __________. (273 years old, 327 years old, 723 years old)
4. When it rained he __________. (climbed into the rubbish bin, got into his rocket, went into the supermarket)

## More to think about

**Write a sentence to answer each question.**

1. Why did the rocket land in the car park?
2. What did the Martian look like?
3. Why did he scuttle behind a rubbish bin?
4. How did the Martian get into the supermarket?

## Now try these

1. Which word in the story means:
   a) broken down
   b) an opening like a small door
   c) very, very
   d) ran with little steps
   e) to twist and turn.
2. Write some sentences about how the Martian feels in this strange new world.
3. Imagine you are in a rocket that has crash-landed on Mars. Write some sentences to explain how you feel and what you can see.

# Unit 11 The Three Billy Goats Gruff

The three Billy Goats Gruff had eaten all the leaves.
They were getting very hungry.

## Do you remember?

**Copy these sentences.**
**Choose a word from the box to fill each gap.**

| stream | leaves | |
|---|---|---|
| three | hungry | troll |

1. There were __________ billy goats.
2. They had eaten all the __________.
3. Now they were feeling very __________.
4. There were more leaves across the __________.
5. An ugly old __________ lived under the bridge.

## More to think about

**Read these sentences about the story.**
**Write 'true', 'false' or 'can't tell' for each one.**

1. The three goats were sisters.
2. They liked beech leaves more than ash leaves.
3. The troll was young.
4. Little Billy Goat Gruff was very hungry.
5. He said he wasn't afraid of the troll.

## Now try these

1. What do you think Little Billy Goat Gruff was feeling when he saw the troll?
2. Write a short introduction to this story about how the troll came to live under the bridge.
3. Write your own ending for the story. Try to make it a surprise.

# Unit 12 Big Bulgy Fat Black Slugs

I don't like
big bulgy fat black slugs.
I don't know why.

When they creep along,
soft and slimy and squashy,
wobbly and wet,
in the long grass;

and when they slide,
their slippery trail
squelchy blobs
along the path;

and when they curl up,
cold and slithery
if I touch one by
mistake;

and when they squidge
between my toes
if I'm running
in bare feet …

that's when I know,
I know for sure,
I wouldn't want one
for a pet.

**Berlie Doherty**

## Do you remember?

**Copy these sentences.**
**Choose a word from the box to fill each gap.**

| pet | slugs | toes | grass | path |
|---|---|---|---|---|

1. The poet doesn't like ___________.
2. She says they are wobbly and wet in the long ___________.
3. They leave their slippery trails along the ___________.
4. She doesn't want them to get between her ___________.
5. She definitely wouldn't want a slug as a ___________.

## More to think about

**Look at the poem again.**
**One word in each sentence is not correct.**
**Write each sentence correctly.**

1. Slugs are usually yellow.
2. They jump through wet grass.
3. When they swim they leave a slippery trail.
4. Slugs explode between your toes.

## Now try these

1. The poet uses words beginning with 's' to describe the slug.
   Make a list of these 's' words.
   Why do you think the poet uses these words?
2. Make a list of your favourite creatures.
   Say why you like each one.
3. Make a list of four creatures you don't like.
   Say what it is you don't like about each one.
4. Imagine the slug could understand English, and heard people saying unkind and rude things about him.
   How would he feel, and what might he say back?

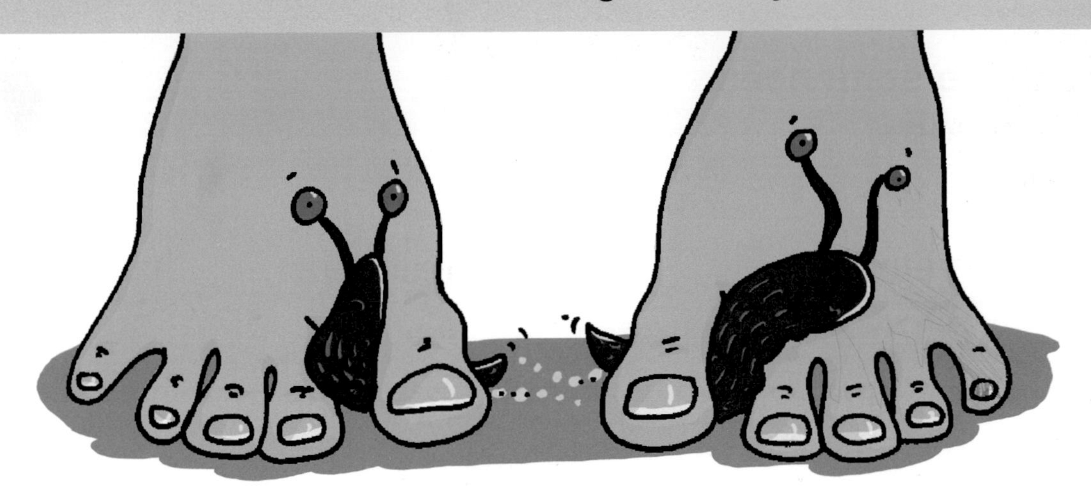

Unit 13

# A Very Busy Day

When someone asks you,
"What did you do today?"
tell them you have been
very, very busy.

After all…
Your hair grew.
Your teeth cut and chewed food.
Your nose smelled smells.
You took in air.
You took goodness from the food you ate.
Your skin stopped germs getting inside you.
Your skeleton moved hundreds of times.
Your muscles moved your bones.
Your heart pumped blood around your body.
Your brain looked after everything you did.

Yes, you and your body have been very busy today!

**Martin Skelton and David Playfoot**

## Do you remember?

**Copy these sentences.**
**Fill each gap.**

1. We need __________ to chew food.
2. Our skin stops __________ getting inside us.
3. __________ move our bones.
4. Our heart pumps __________ around our body.

## More to think about

**Read these sentences.**
**Write 'true' or 'not true' for each one.**

1. Our hair is growing all the time.
2. We take in air through our ears.
3. We must eat food to live.
4. All the bones in our bodies make our skeletons.
5. Our brains are very important.

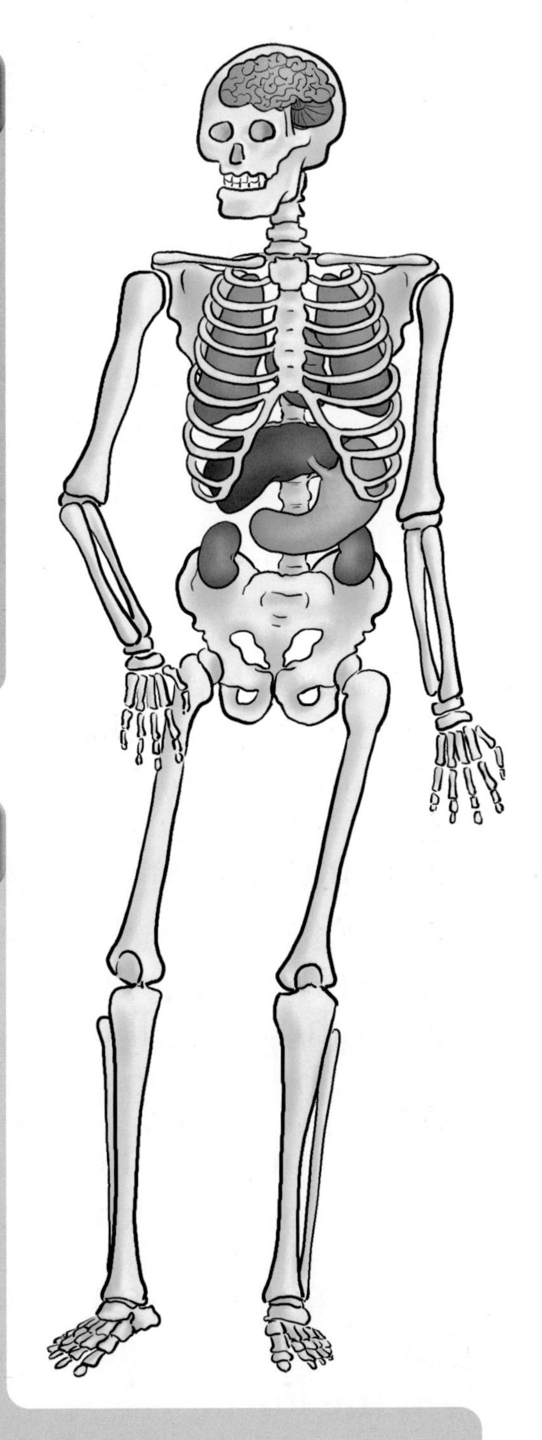

## Now try these

1. Copy these lists next to each other. Match the body parts to the senses they control.

| | |
|---|---|
| skin | sight |
| nose | hearing |
| ears | touch |
| tongue | smell |
| eyes | taste |

2. Make a list of five rules to help you keep healthy. One has been done to help you.

   1. Always wash your hands before eating food.

3. 'A Very Busy Day' is about how your body is busy every day. Write a list of the things that still happen when you are asleep at night.

# Two Legs or Four?

Ben wanted the new puppy to have the same name as him.

"It's going to be very confusing," said Dad.

In fact, as time went by, they found it rather useful to have both the son and dog with the same name. Ben spent all day with Ben, and the same words served for both.

"Be quiet, Ben!" for instance, stopped one yelling and the other yapping, and both came when the name was called, and sat down when they were ordered, and each looked equally pleased when told "What a good boy, Ben!"

And indeed Ben was a good boy or rather a good puppy. He never made messes on the carpet, he never chewed the curtains or covers, he ate well and he slept soundly at night. As well as learning the ordinary things that dogs learn, he took to copying everything the boy did.

If Ben laughed, Ben barked. If Ben cried, Ben howled. If Ben lost his temper and roared angrily, Ben growled.

And one day, would you believe it, Mum looked out of the window to see not one, but two Bens turning somersaults on the lawn.

**Dick King-Smith**

## Do you remember?

**Write the correct answer to each question.**

1. What new pet did the family have?
   a) They had a kitten.
   b) They had a puppy.
2. Who wanted the new pet to be called Ben?
   a) Mum wanted to call it Ben.
   b) Ben wanted to call it Ben.
3. How did the puppy behave?
   a) It was a good puppy.
   b) It was a naughty puppy.
4. Did the puppy mess on the carpets?
   a) Yes, the puppy messed on the carpets.
   b) No, the puppy never messed on the carpets.

## More to think about

1. Write a sentence to answer each question.
   a) Why was it useful to have the boy and the puppy with the same name?
   b) What did the puppy do when the boy laughed?
   c) What did the puppy do when the boy lost his temper?
2. Find words in the story that mean:
   a) becoming mixed up
   b) shouting
   c) giving an order
   d) the same amount
   e) crossly
   f) rolling head-over-heels.

## Now try these

1. Why do you think the puppy copied everything the boy did?
2. Pretend that you have just been given a new pet.
   Write about how you feel and how you will look after it.
3. Do you think there would be problems caused by the boy and the dog having the same name?
   Explain your answer and give some examples.